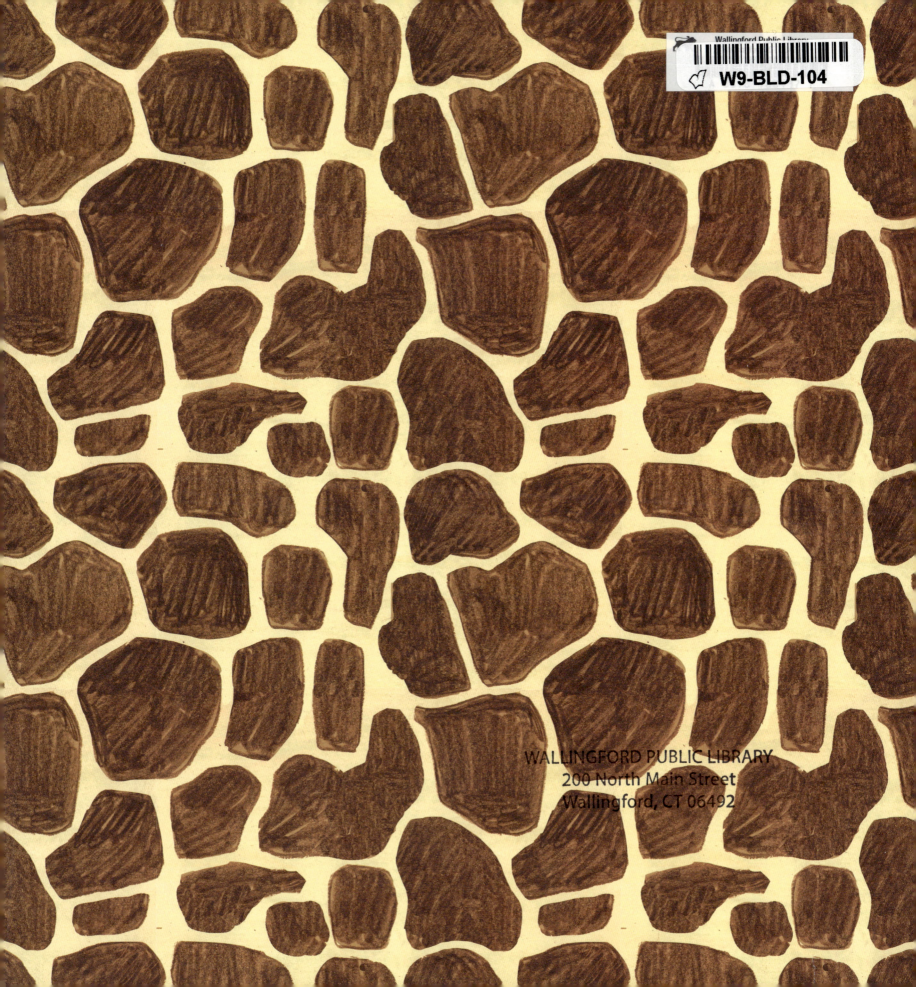

For my family, in its many forms—RH

For my family, a curiosity of Joneses—KJ

To Annabella, Owen, and Charlotte—newest additions
to the zany Durst family!—KD

W

PENGUIN WORKSHOP
Penguin Young Readers Group
An Imprint of Penguin Random House LLC

Text copyright © 2018 by Penguin Random House LLC. Illustrations copyright © 2018 by Kathryn Durst. All rights reserved.
Published by Penguin Workshop, an imprint of Penguin Random House LLC, 345 Hudson Street, New York, New York 10014.
PENGUIN and PENGUIN WORKSHOP are trademarks of Penguin Books Ltd, and the W colophon is a trademark
of Penguin Random House LLC. Manufactured in China.

Library of Congress Cataloging-in-Publication Data is available.

ISBN 9781524789374   10 9 8 7 6 5 4 3 2 1

LIFE WITH MY FAMILY

by Renee Hooker & Karl Jones
illustrated by Kathryn Durst

Penguin Workshop
An Imprint of Penguin Random House

So sometimes I wonder
what *else* we could be...

As a pod of pelicans,
we'd soar above trees.

No time to fight as a busy swarm of bees.

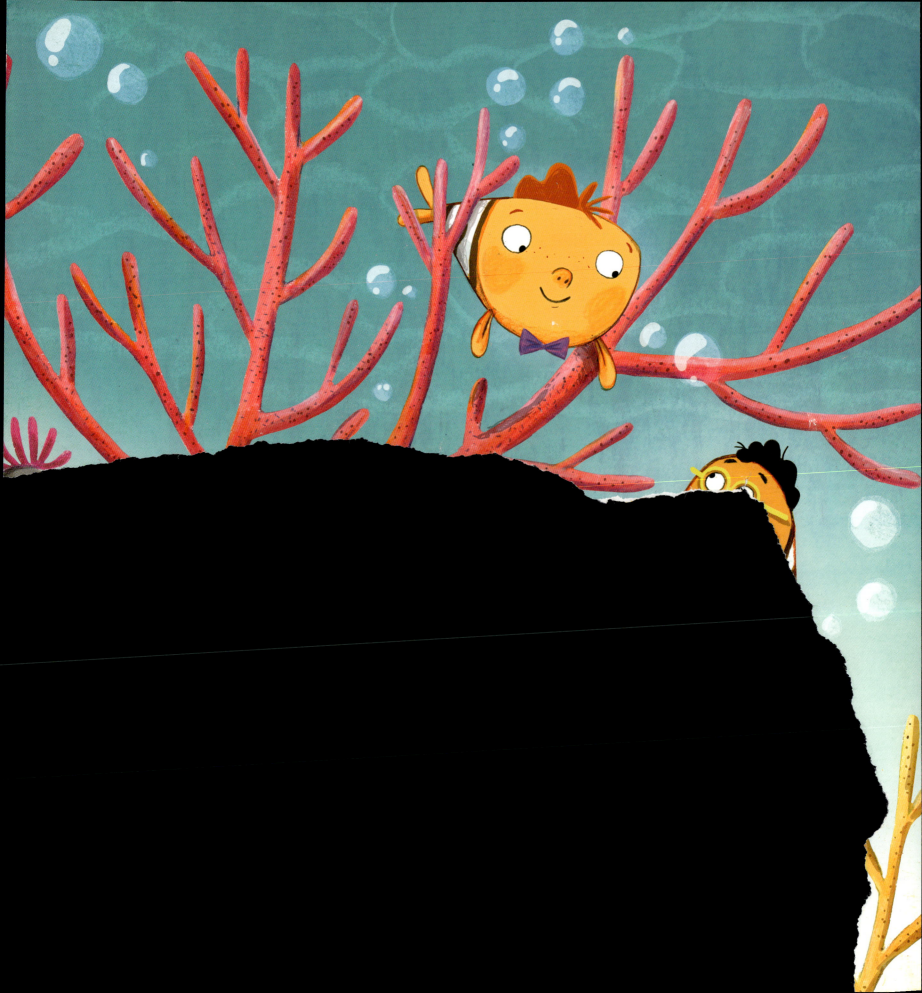

As a school of fish,
we'd swim among the bubbles.

As a herd of buffalo,
flies would be our only troubles.

As a playful pride of lions,
we'd hunt and we'd trap.

As a pandemonium of parrots,
we'd squawk and we'd flap.

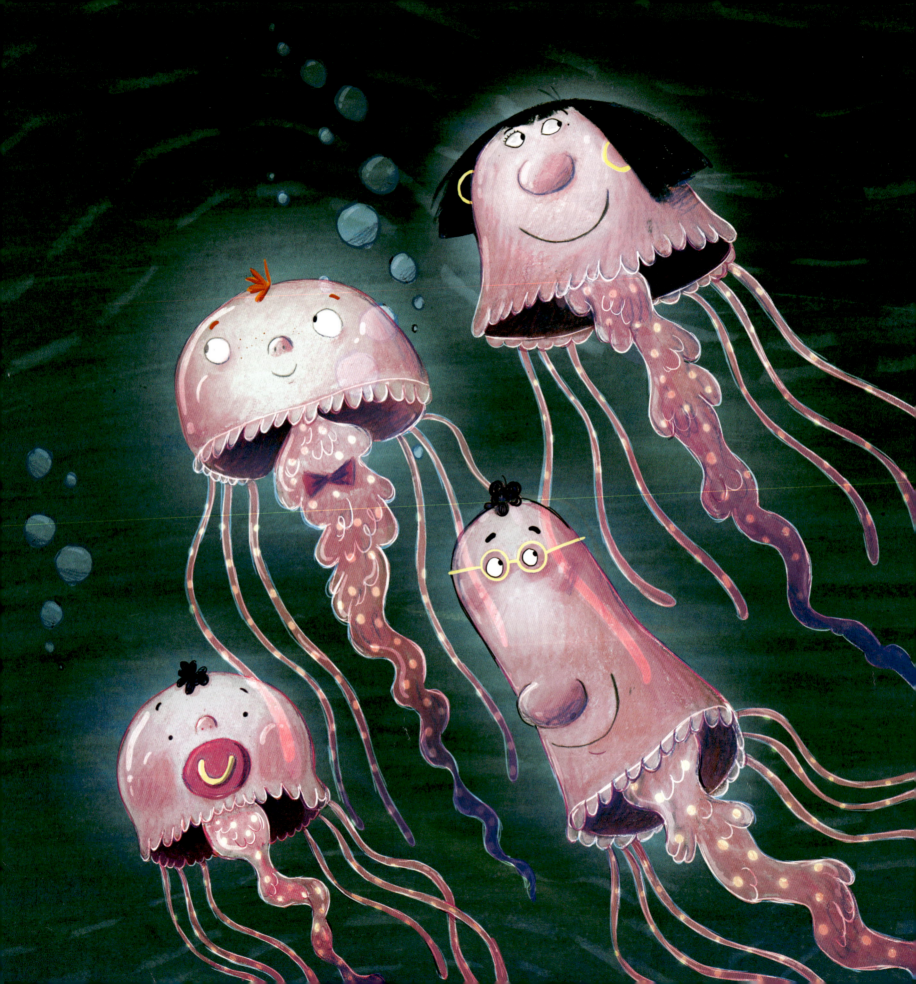

As a smack of jellyfish,
we'd float, clear as glass.

As a wisdom of wombats,
We'd waddle through grass.

But as animals, I guess
we might have problems, too...

What if they tried to take my little brother to the zoo?!

Life isn't always easy with my family...

But while we're together,
there's nowhere else I'd rather be.

For hundreds of years, humans have used collective nouns to describe groups of different animals. This story contains a few examples of those collective nouns, also called "terms of venery." Here is a list of even more words you can use to describe groups of animals.

A troop of baboons
A murder of crows
A pod of dolphins
A convocation of eagles
A busyness of ferrets
A journey of giraffes
A cloud of grasshoppers
A bloat of hippopotamuses

A mess of iguanas
A litter of kittens
A leap of leopards
A scourge of mosquitoes
A watch of nightingales
A parliament of owls

A colony of penguins
A crash of rhinoceroses
A cluster of spiders
An ambush of tigers
A nest of vipers
A descent of woodpeckers
A zeal of zebras